Drabble Harvest:
Haunted Spaceports

Edited by Terrie Leigh Relf

DRABBLE HARVEST IS EDITED BY TERRIE LEIGH RELF

All rights reserved. No part of this book may be reproduced or transmitted in any form or by any means, electronic or mechanical, including photo-copying or recording or by any information storage and retrieval systems, without expressed written consent of the author and/or artists. Any similarity between places and persons mentioned in the fiction or semi-fiction and real places or persons living or dead is coincidental.

Story copyrights owned by the respective authors

Cover Art "Haunted" by t.santitoro
Cover design by Marcia A. Borell

Drabble Harvest is published three times a year, in conjunction with The Hiraeth Publishing Drabble Contests

Contents

5 A Little Help, Please
10 Editorial by Terrie Leigh Relf
11 Spaceport *Echo-Nine* by Tom Duke
12 Dropped G by Marcia A. Borell
13 Their Special Spot by Francis W. Alexander
18 Haunted Spaceports by A. Zaykova
20 Empty by DJ Tyrer
21 The Unlucky Seven by Debby Feo
24 Flight of Fear by Denise Hatfield
25 Outer Limits by Denise Hatfield
28 Atlantis by Katherine Relf-Canas
29 Lost in the Dark by Paul Lewthwaite
30 Sacrifice by Jay Kleem
31 Standby by Greg Schwartz
34 Hell Is an Eternal Loop by Jeff Currier
36 Death on the Horizon by Lee Andrew Forman
37 The Departure by William R Brimer
39 The Song of Ghosts by Matthew Wilson
40 Riley's Tavern by K. A. Williams
41 Vengeance by Randall Andrews
44 I'm a Believer by t.santitoro
45 The Maternity Ward by Gary Davis

SALE AT HIRAETH PUBLISHING!!!

THERE'S A SALE GOING ON!!! IT'S STILL GOING ON!!!

BUY ALL THE BOOKS YOU WANT AND USE THIS 20% DISCOUNT CODE:

BOOKS2023

GO TO OUR SHOP AT
WWW.HIRAETHSFFH.COM

NO MASKS, NO WAITING, AND WE NEVER CLOSE!

From the desk of the deputy assistant adjutant to the Boortean Ambassador

A Little Help, Please

In the world of the small indie press we fight a never-ending battle for attention to our work, as writers and in publishing. Here's an example: big publishers [you know who they are] have gobs of $$$ that they can devote to advertising and marketing. Here at Hiraeth Publishing, our advertising budget consists of the deposits for whatever soda bottles and aluminum cans we can find alongside the highways. Anti-littering laws make our task even more difficult . . . ☺

That's where YOU come in. YOU are our best promoter. YOU are the one who can tell others about us. Just send 'em to our website, tell them about our store. That's all. Just that.

Of course, we don't mind if you talk us up. We're pretty good, you know. We have some award-winning and award-nominated writers and artists, plus other voices well-deserving to be heard [not everyone wins awards, right?] but our publications are read-worthy nevertheless.

That number once again is:
www.hiraethsffh.com

Friend us on Facebook at Hiraeth Publish

Follow us on Twitter at @HiraethPublish1

Iuliae: Past Tense
By Tyree Campbell

Two sisters of the Iulius Family have run away from the restrictions and rules of their settlement on a remote world, and embark on a journey of discovery, to learn what to do with their new-found freedom. Along the way, they become smugglers, and opponents of human trafficking, and become fugitives from the law and from the corporations.

Iulia Sexta, the younger of the two sisters, is suffering from an identity crisis. Is it gender dysphoria? Was she supposed to be a man? Is that why she likes girls? Or is a ghost from one of her previous lives now trying to haunt his way back into the living by taking over her body and mind?

With both the past and the present pursuing them, Iulia Tertia and Iulia Sexta find their future under constant attack. Doing the right thing is not only difficult at best, but may well result in their deaths. What to do? One thing at a time...

Order and read the adventure of a lifetime!

https://www.hiraethsffh.com/product-page/iuliae-past-tense-by-tyree-campbell

The Sisterhood of the Blood Moon
By Terrie Leigh Relf

For thousands of Earth years, the Transgalactic Consortium has had an invested interest in this planet and its inhabitants, the Haurans. While the Sisterhood of the Blood Moon and the Guardians work together with the Consortium and Haurans to restore balance to the universe, the Blood Moon is fast approaching. The power of this moon reveals untold secrets . . . including the sacred covenant with the Mora Spiders. There is an ancient pact that continues to be honored – but at what cost and for whose purpose?

The world may come to an end. But will there be a chance for a new beginning? And if so, where?

Find out! Order a copy now!

https://www.hiraethsffh.com/product-page/sisterhood-of-the-blood-moon-by-terrie-leigh-relf from the desk of the Boortean Ambassador . . .

Greetings Space Travelers!

Welcome aboard our trans-galactic and trans-dimensional spaceport. We hope you enjoy your stay. Whether you're en route to another station or will be here for the duration, we are here to serve you. There have been rumors that our space station is haunted. While there may be some evidence to support this, investigations are still underway. That said, we sincerely hope that you will maintain an open mind and appreciate the many services that we have to offer. Safe journey for those of you who are heading through the portal or on to other posts.

As always, please join me in thanking the individuals who are reporting their experiences.

Until next time,
Your humble ambassador,
Terrie Leigh Relf

Spaceport *Echo-Niner*
Tom Duke

We've arrived! Can't say I enjoyed the confines of our small ship. But the port change will do me good. The people on SPE-8 were becoming a bore. SPE-9 is bigger than I imagined. More people. More opportunities to make acquaintances. Maybe a secret friend. Our transport brought just twelve. And me, of course. Lucky 13. I'll begin exploring the port immediately. Every corridor, cabin, and crevice. Invading all the intimate spaces of my new port mates. You know, make myself at home. This is, after all, *my* new haunt.

—From the journal of Spytz, the Gypsy Cat Space Ghost

Dropped G
Marcia A. Borell

Fearless Fighters, that's what the boss named our company. We've battled mutant bugs, alien invasive plants, and even walking land sharks. Big blasters, fog exterminators, and web stickers were our primary tools.

What was The Boss thinking? Our orders: Get rid of the hosts. Maybe it was biological.

Half of the spaceport had been abandoned. The Boss Deep-Space-Networked us as we suited up. Why was he using the DSN? That com was ancient history. He said to enter through the abandoned portal and keep our suits on. The slime was toxic, and the ghosts were nasty.

GHOSTS! WE'RE NOT PREPARED!

Their Special Spot
Francis W. Alexander

I sit near the window and look for them. My ship doesn't leave for another ten minutes.

As the story goes, Spaceport Genesis was bombed with a tremendous loss of life. The authorities turned it into a memorial. Since this is the best spot in the system for a spaceport, the authorities built this spaceport around Genesis which is still frequented by the ghostly travelers.

Rising to leave, I see a kid. They never interact with us. It appears he's looking directly at me. I wave. He returns the favor which freaks me out as I head for the exit.

When the Mushrooms Come
By Francis W. Alexander

The Atomic Age brought with it many wonders and great strides forward. It also brought nuclear war. We often forget how many nuclear warheads are still scattered about our world, and how many countries are still trying to make their own. What would happen to ordinary people if one fell without warning? Follow along in the lives of different people as they move through the drop of a nuclear bomb – before, during, and after the fall. See their lives before the flash, their reactions when the mushroom cloud rises, and how the survivors struggle on.

https://www.hiraethsffh.com/product-page/when-the-mushrooms-come-by-francis-w-alexander

Skellies:
A Coloring Book
By Marcia A. Borell

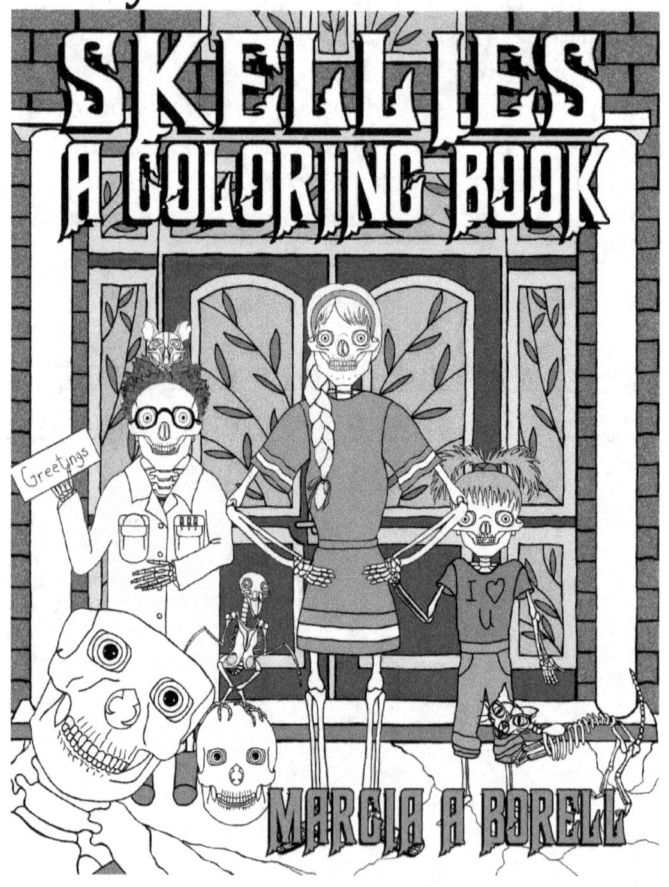

Greetings Colorists, Journal Keepers, and Skelly Lovers

Welcome to my warped world of beloved skellies. We all have our own personal skeletons, which enable us to get from here to there.

I hope that you will spend some time decorating and adding designs to these skellies. They are often wayward, a little bit rowdy, sometimes ridiculous, and occasionally bad to the bone. They are not very scary. I grew up next to a cemetery where we had many dead that would drop by for a visit. Most of them wanted to share their story, which had ended too abruptly for them.

I hope that they will make you laugh and groan in a good-natured way. You may even recognize that one or more of them will remind you of someone you know.

https://www.hiraethsffh.com/product-page/skellies-a-coloring-book-by-marcia-a-borell

First Place

Haunted Spaceports
A. Zaykova

He sold their house and left the planet, hoping to forget her. But when he landed on Xing11, there she was, sipping coffee in the spaceport's lounge. Later, he glimpsed her in the streets, in the windows of shops, and in the artificial park outside his new workplace. He took off again and again; she was waiting for him at the terminal. His life became a kaleidoscope of ever-changing jobs, spaceships, and planets. He'd thought the court ruling him innocent would've cleared his conscience. But as he ran through these haunted spaceports, he couldn't shake the weight of her death.

And NOW a word from our newest sponsor (Brought to YOU by The Boortean Ambassador)

Tertu's Medium Service

Have you been experiencing strange phenomena? Perhaps your spaceport's crew and guests have experienced one or more of the following:

- Missing items
- Hearing voices
- Feeling cold spots
- Sensing that they're being watched
- Seeing people appear or disappear

If so, there may be ghosts in residence. While some spirits may be benign and perhaps mischievous, others may be malicious and harmful. Rather than speculate, contact Tertu's Medium Service for a consultation. She and her staff will determine whether your spaceport is being haunted and will contact the spirits to reach an agreement or release them to the Four Corners and beyond!

Empty
DJ Tyrer

No life detected by planetary scans, but Starport's automated systems still worked just fine, so we put in, hoping to refuel.

Waiting for the automated fuelling rig to finish, some of us decided to go take a look about, stretch our legs. Still appeared inhabited, but with no signs of anyone alive; no bodies, either.

But, just out of sight, there'd be sounds—footsteps, doors shutting like somebody was there.

Perhaps just robots we saw none but, when we lifted off, the ship's computer kept registering empty rooms occupied and objects would move when unwatched, and I had to wonder . . .

The Unlucky Seven
Debby Feo

The launchpad was currently occupied by the seven spirits of all who had died during the mishap with the solid fuel rocket. Unfortunately, some very important people, including the Governor of Asteroid101, had been in the old fashioned crew capsule, which had been requisitioned for the memorial flight.

No one was still alive on Earth or on Asteroid101c, who had firsthand experience with any kind of solid fuel rocket. One tiny missing screw plate allowed the oxidizer to mix prematurely with the fuel.

The Unlucky Seven were understandably enraged at the oversight. They haunted anyone who came near the launchpad.

Living Bad Dreams
By Denise Hatfield

When dreams come alive, there's no telling where they will lead. Everything changes when you realize that, dream or no dream, you're going to die. What do you do then?

Type: Novella
Audience: adults

Ordering Link:
Print Edition ($9.00):
https://www.hiraethsffh.com/product-page/living-bad-dreams-by-denise-hatfield-1

ePub Edition ($2.99):
https://www.hiraethsffh.com/product-page/living-bad-dreams-by-denise-hatfield-2

PDF Edition ($2.99):
https://www.hiraethsffh.com/product-page/living-bad-dreams-by-denise-hatfield

Flight Of Fear
Denise Hatfield

I followed her through Port 18. The only person I had seen in two years. She pointed to the map of the Launch Stations. I trailed behind, as we passed a family frozen in stasis pods. She put a finger to her lips.

Why isn't she talking?

The loading bay was brightly lit and alive with the hum of electricity. We climbed into the shuttle and strapped into the seatbelts.

"Where are we going?" I asked over the loud noise of the arriving shuttle. I turned to look at blank space. Alone. The passenger seatbelts lay untouched except my own.

Outer Limits
Denise Hatfield

The shuttle throbbed with energy. The launch sign above the endless dark opening blipped on as I tried to release the belts. Whatever was holding the shuttle released with a loud *Clunk*, and I was blasted ahead. My heart and stomach were left back in the bay. The smell of ozone, metal, and electricity was an overload on my senses. As swirls of rainbow-colored lights wrapped, flipped, and rolled me, with a sudden jerk, it was over quickly. I was met by a twirling fog. The fog was screaming . . . thousands of soulless eyes . . . so many teeth. The Damned were hungry.

Authors Note: These are influenced by a roller coaster called the Outer Limits: Flight of Fear built in 1996 at Kings Island in Mason, Ohio. The Outer Limits part was dropped in 2001. It has an alien theme based off of the TV show, *Outer Limits*. A ride I still enjoy. If you're ever in town, ride if you dare.

INDIGO

By Tyree Campbell

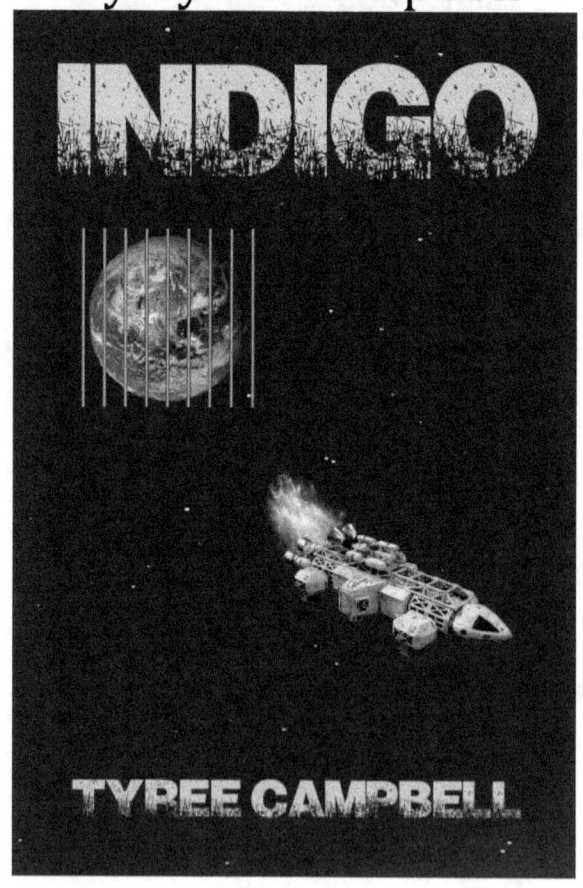

Matt has a special gift that will enable him to avenge his brother's death. Kerise has another use for that talent, if only she can persuade him to abandon his personal quest and help her with a project called Indigo.

Echelon, a secret government project, also wants Matt because of his gift. But as he and other like him cannot be controlled, they pose a threat to national security. Orders go out to have them eliminated.

Interpol is on the lookout for Kerise and for the Indigo project. There is no place on Earth where Matt and Kerise and her associates will be safe. Nowhere on Earth...but they cannot be safe unless Matt commits himself to Indigo. And he's not about to do that...

https://www.hiraethsffh.com/product-page/indigo-by-tyree-campbell

Atlantis
Katherine Relf-Canas

Legend has it that when the mission first arrived here, half its crew waded into the breakers of the so-called Atlantic Ocean, named for the one on Earth that it so resembled.

After an hour, the crew's bones began to dissolve. They weren't dead. They had regressed–into animals without backbones. Their skin sacks intact, they learned to move and speak, from whence came new branches of English. Now, it's the planet's second official language.

They say they're still down there. Could be the next generation. Some think it's the ghosts of the crew disturbing the waters.

Look, over there!

Lost in the Dark
Paul Lewthwaite

Radio comms were down, but Beth staggered to her feet, scanning her suit's readout for distress signals. *What the hell had just happened?*

She limped to the spaceport's maintenance airlock. *Weird. No overhead traffic.* She opened the outer hatch and gasped.

Pitch black. Dead.

* * *

"Airlock one, inner doors opening," said the young officer. "No override possible! Ambient temperature dropping . . . Ma'am, there's no one there!"

"Easy, lad," replied Commander Rayner.

The same pattern every year for the past ten since the explosion. No one wanted to work down there. She couldn't blame them.

A woman's haunting sobs crackled over the intercom.

Sacrifice
Jay Kleem

You're doing something noble when you activate the self-destruct sequence. Stoic, you think of the loved ones you leave behind and your rapidly dissipating future now unstoppably written by your own trembling finger. *Someone* needed to prevent this bastard ship from claiming new victims in distant galaxies. And because of a short straw, that someone was you.

KA-BOOM!

You regain consciousness, not in Heaven, but trapped forever in the reconstructed bowels of the spaceport's haunted hull. You then realize the ship manipulated you, like it did its other phantoms. And, like them, you too are now angry at the living.

Standby
Greg Schwartz

Another flight took off with a roar. Jarvis glanced around and checked his watch. He felt like he'd been waiting forever. Beings of all shapes and sizes hustled past.
Maybe he'd make it on the next flight...

* * *

The terminal was full, but Bleena spotted an empty seat a few rows down. She hurried over, bags in tow.
As she approached the seat, a strange coldness emanated from it. Almost tangible, it settled around her like a damp shawl. Bleena shivered and backed away.
She slumped against the wall and closed her eyes.
Maybe she'd make it on the next flight...

In Days to Come
By Lisa Timpf

The poems in this collection are grouped into four sections. The first, "Terra, Terra," includes poems set on the planet Earth. That is true of many of the poems in the second section, "Looming Shadows," though they have been grouped together in relation to some of the potential disasters we as a human race have set ourselves up for—nuclear warfare, climate change, and so on. "Alien Encounters" contains poems relating to imagined interactions with other space-faring species. "Other Worlds" rounds out the collection with speculations on what life might be like if and when humanity spins out to the stars.

https://www.hiraethsffh.com/product-page/in-days-to-come-by-lisa-timpf

Honorable Mention

Hell is an Eternal Loop
Jeff Currier

We're screwed!
Why?
Space station *Ouroboros* keeps looping back in time.
So?
So each jump resets the whole universe—us with it.
Can we stop it?
Unlikely. We're too far away, so not enough time.

* * *

We're so screwed!
Why?
Space station *Ouroboros* keeps looping back in time.
Can we stop it?
Hmmm, let me check the tachyon decay differentials—nope, definitely not enough time.

* * *

We're sooo . . . screwed!
Why?
Space station *Ouroboros* keeps looping back in time.
So?
Each jump resets the universe.
Can we stop it?
Not without divine intervention—the loop is too short.
How long?
666 seconds.
Damn!

Death on the Horizon
Lee Andrew Forman

As I roam the empty corridors of Horizon-53, I wonder where everyone has gone. Once, it was filled with life, ships docked and undocked, their weary travelers chattered between journeys. Now it is occupied only by myself and my wandering thoughts. I don't know how long it has been since anyone came to this quiet port. I can't seem to remember; when you're alone in the same place time loses meaning. It must affect memory as well. I can't recall the last time I've eaten. But I don't feel hunger. Only the loneliness that has drawn out for so long.

The Departure
William R Brimer

When the duo's freighter docked, random scorched debris — suspended in the port's atmosphere — rattled across the ship's surface. A charred leg bone floated in zero gravity outside the cockpit.

"Boss," Dwight said. "Let's hightail."

"Negative," Willard said. "No fuel. Suit up."

They suited and departed. Shadows skittered across the port. Dwight connected the fuel line. Willard scanned for life. There was none.

A mutilated, headless spacesuit stood magnetized and swaying. Its arms hovered. Further out on the landing, another just like it.

"What do you figure happened here?" Dwight said.

"This is strange," Willard said. "The scanner isn't detecting us."

And NOW a word from a new sponsor . . . (Brought to YOU by the Boortean Ambassador)

Roda's Spaceport Cleaning and Cleansing Services

If your spaceport is being haunted, there's an excellent chance that many spirits are making a mess. There's also an excellent chance that your staff and guests are too, particularly if they're caught off guard, startled, or otherwise frightened by these phenomena. Under these circumstances, staff may not be fulfilling their duties.

In addition to basic spaceport cleaning (which includes, but is not limited to, hygiene alcoves, kitchens, and common areas), we provide protection spells. Furthermore, we have access to state-of-the-art portal technology for those instances where a simple banishing spell isn't effective.

Contact us NOW for a complimentary consultation!

Second Place

The Song of Ghosts
Matthew Wilson

I run a clean establishment. There's no drinking in my spaceport, no fighting, and certainly no ghosts. Interstellar pilots want a drink after their long journey through the stars, but since that damn ship docked here, their ratings on my social media page have plunged.

Sometimes, bodies are found in the boosters and the lucky ones still have their heads, but I don't believe in curses. Guests complain of nightmares, and I tell myself they put themselves out of airlocks to stop their depression, not the songs of ghosts.

Either way, I wish the *S.S. Mary Celeste* hadn't docked here.

Riley's Tavern
K.A. Williams

The *Santa Maria* docked at Orion Twelve and her crew disembarked. Jackson and Cutter hurried to the nearest bar. "Give us a whiskey," Jackson said to the barmaid.

"I can't. Pirates hijacked the supply freighter. There won't be another one in this sector for weeks. If you want a drink bad enough, you can go to Riley's Tavern."

Cutter frowned. "What do you think?"

Jackson shrugged. "They're just rumors, let's go see for ourselves."

* * *

Jackson and Cutter stepped inside the bar. Glasses filled themselves at the tap and floated around. The pair exchanged glances and sat at an empty table.

Honorable Mention

Vengeance
Randall Andrews

It took me three days to reach base camp—three days from where my mutinous crew left me for dead. Where my frozen body remains.

For the next week, I stood staring at my favorite coffee mug, still resting on the shelf where I left it. Much of that time, the crew went about their business around me, oblivious to my presence. Day and night, I glared at that cup, focusing all my hate and anger upon it, willing it to move.

And finally, it did.

Now I've shifted my gaze to the airlock release. I will have my revenge.

Those Who Die
by t.santitoro

A young nobleman's first sexual encounter is arranged by his father, to couple with a sentient plant being, a flauna-form. The youth unexpectedly falls in love with the plant/animal girl, and becomes totally addicted to her, fully knowing that—like the rest of her species—she only has one day to live.

When the object of his love at last roots herself to her home planet and becomes comatose for all eternity, the young man finds himself trapped in a state of incurable loss, unable to get her out of his mind.

Just by chance, he later discovers part of the flauna-form clinging to his clothes, and plants the leaf in his garden at home, tending a new version of flauna-form, hoping to one day find —and be reunited with—his lost beloved.

This is a story of tragedy, danger and moral decline, a Frankenstein-esque tale of creating that which threatens one's very existence.

https://www.hiraethsffh.com/product-page/those-who-die-by-t-santitoro

I'm a Believer
t.santitoro

I had never believed in ghosts, but lately, things aboard the spaceport had begun to get weird.

Items had gone missing, strange sounds had been heard in the dark, perfumed scents had wafted through empty corridors, indistinct figures appeared to walk through bulkheads, and objects had moved without being touched.

None of these events had happened directly to me or my property, and I had easily dismissed them out of hand. I had actually scoffed at the gullible personnel who had reported them.

Until I was working in the airlock, and the hatch began to cycle open all by itself.

The Maternity Ward
Gary Davis

Captain Nathan Albert Wilcox was born in a spaceport orbiting Jupiter. His parents died when he was a baby. He was raised in three orphanages circling various planets. Nathan was now zooming towards Neptune. Suddenly, although his spaceship appeared unaffected, Nathan felt the sensation of being turned upside down and then immediately right-side up. Dizzy, he nevertheless continued to the next spaceport. Entering, Nathan noticed a maternity ward straight ahead. He saw one baby sleeping in the Infants Recovery Room. The newborn's nameplate read: "Nathan Albert Wilcox." Shocked, Nathan looked up at the window and saw his parents. "Mom, Dad!"

And NOW a word from our most-esteemed sponsor . . . (Brought to YOU by the Boortean Ambassador)

Assistants Needed at T'Lar's Podling Care Center

That right. T'lar have three podlings now. He experience strange feelings when born. Not want to leave podlings' side. That okay because T'lar now house husband and smart life partner run businesses with cousins. So, T'lar have thoughts. He open Podling Care Center. Podlings play together when older. Podlings learn together when older. So many nappies. Podlings hungry all the time. When not sleeping, podlings like singing and funny faces and mobiles that go round and round. T'lar need help. T'lar not sleep much. T'lar not eat much. T'lar not take shower. Call now for interview. Good pay. Good hours.